D1533380

To Lappi
—N.K.

To Antonio Salieri
—H.W.

LITTLE SIMON
Simon & Schuster Building, Rockefeller Center
1230 Avenue of the Americas, New York, New York 10020
Text copyright © 1994 by Nurit Karlin.
Illustrations copyright © 1994 by Hans Wilhelm.
Also available in a SIMON & SCHUSTER BOOKS FOR YOUNG READERS
hardcover edition. All rights reserved including the right
of reproduction in whole or in any part in any form.
Designed by David Neuhaus.
Manufactured in Mexico

10 9 8 7 6 5 4 3 2

ISBN: 0-671-88601-0 (pbk)
ISBN: 0-671-88026-8

Ten Little Bunnies

by Nurit Karlin · illustrated by Hans Wilhelm

LITTLE SIMON
Published by Simon & Schuster
New York   London   Toronto   Sydney   Tokyo   Singapore

They'll never see us back here.

BUNNY POWER

and then there were nine.

Nine little bunnies hopped through a gate.
Hippity hop, one couldn't stop...

BONK!

and then there were eight.

Eight little bunnies looked up to heaven.
Bzz! Bzz! What did they see? A busy bumblebee...

STING!

and then there were seven.

Seven little bunnies carried some bricks.
That wasn't easy, one felt so queasy...

and then there were six.

Six little bunnies went for a drive.
Vroom, vroom, a witch on a broom...

SWEEP!

and then there were five.

SLAM!

and then there were four.

Four little bunnies climbed up a tree.
Way, way up, a flying saucer and a cup...

OOSH!

and then there were three.

HEEELP!

and then there were two.

Two little bunnies ate bun after bun.
Yummy! Yummy! One stuffed his tummy...

BOOM!

and then there was one.

One little bunny, alone in a nook,
with one little stick and one magic trick...

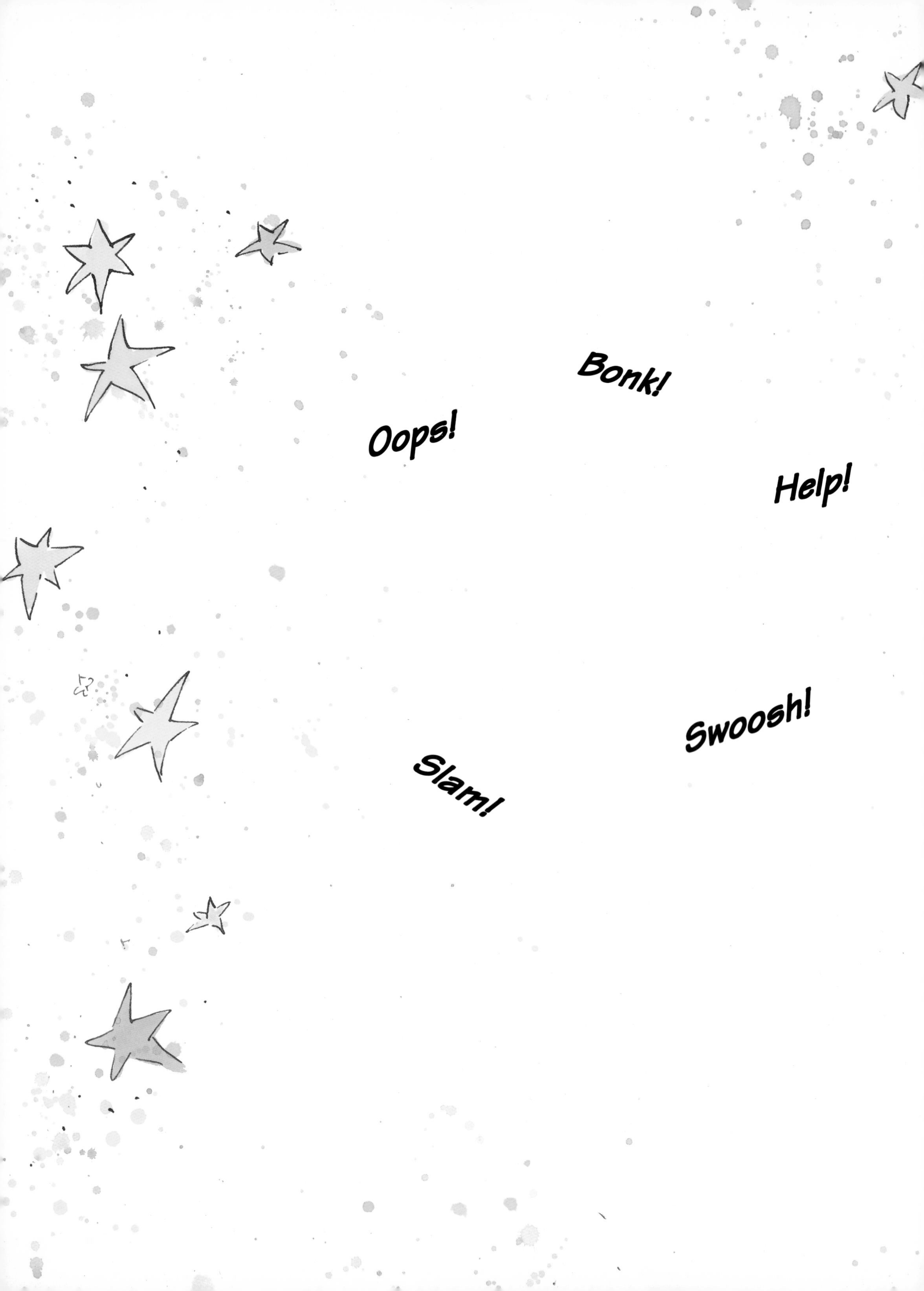
Bonk!
Oops!
Help!
Swoosh!
Slam!

Whoosh!

Crash!

Sting!

Boom!

And look!